WITHDRAWN

the CRitteR club

Liz's Pie in the Sky

by Callie Barkley ♥ illustrated by Tracy Bishop

LITTLE SIMON
New York   London   Toronto   Sydney   New Delhi

LITTLE SIMON

An imprint of Simon & Schuster Children's Publishing Division · 1230 Avenue of the Americas, New York, New York 10020 · First Little Simon hardcover edition October 2021. Copyright © 2021 by Simon & Schuster, Inc. All rights reserved, including the right of reproduction in whole or in part in any form.

LITTLE SIMON is a registered trademark of Simon & Schuster, Inc., and associated colophon is a trademark of Simon & Schuster, Inc. For information about special discounts for bulk purchases, please contact Simon & Schuster Special Sales at 1-866-506-1949 or business@simonandschuster.com.

The Simon & Schuster Speakers Bureau can bring authors to your live event. For more information or to book an event contact the Simon & Schuster Speakers Bureau at 1-866-248-3049 or visit our website at www.simonspeakers.com.

Designed by Brittany Fetcho.

Manufactured in the United States of America 0821 FFG 10 9 8 7 6 5 4 3 2 1

Cataloging-in-Publication Data is available for this title from the Library of Congress.

ISBN 978-1-5344-8712-3 (hc)

ISBN 978-1-5344-8711-6 (pbk)

ISBN 978-1-5344-8713-0 (ebook)

Table of Contents

chapter 1

Recipe for Fun

Liz Jenkins was the first to the lunch table. She sat down closest to the cafeteria windows. Outside, there was a large maple tree. Each day, more of its leaves were golden yellow. Liz smiled. Fall was her favorite time of year.

Liz's friends Marion and Amy sat down next.

"That spelling test was hard," said Amy. "Wasn't it?"

It was Friday. Like every Friday, their teacher, Mrs. Sienna, had quizzed them on their spelling words right before lunch.

"Lots of those words had silent letters," Marion replied as she unwrapped her bagel. "But I think I got them all."

Liz nodded. That sounded about right. Marion almost always got 100 percent on spelling tests.

Ellie was last to the lunch table.

"Did anybody know the bonus word?" Ellie asked them with a frown. "Cornucopia?"

"I did!" Liz replied. "That's a horn-shaped basket thing. We always put one on our Thanksgiving buffet."

Liz was the artsy one in her house. So she was always in charge of decorating for Thanksgiving. She filled the cornucopia with small pumpkins and gourds in wacky shapes. Plus some red and green apples for color.

Liz sighed. She gazed out again at the golden maple tree. She loved everything about fall. The leaves. The weather.

And *especially* trips to Marigold Lake!

Liz's family had a cabin there. And that very weekend, Liz's friends were coming up to stay!

Before long, the spelling test was old news. The girls were excited about their autumn getaway.

"Remember the last time we were all there?" Liz asked her friends. "Roasting marshmallows over the campfire?"

Ellie giggled. "Remember that stick I thought was a snake?"

"And how I flipped the canoe?" Amy said, blushing a little bit.

"And the baby mice?" Marion added.

"Awwwww," all the girls said together. They had found several teeny, tiny baby mice in the cabin. But there had been no mama mouse in sight.

Luckily for the mice, the girls had a safe place to take them. It was their very own animal rescue shelter, The Critter Club. The four of them ran the shelter with the help of Amy's mom, a veterinarian. Dr. Purvis helped the girls care for the baby mice until they were big enough to be released into the wild.

"That *was* a good weekend," Liz said. "And this one will be too!"

Liz grinned. She had something planned.

This Thanksgiving, Liz was in charge of making one of the Thanksgiving pies. She had already picked out the flavor: cranberry-blueberry pie with a hint of orange and cinnamon. Liz wanted it to be perfect. So she needed to practice. She was going to start this weekend at the cabin. And Amy, Marion, and Ellie could help.

Suddenly, Liz had a thought. Rather than having the girls help, they could each make a pie of their own. This was going to be the best surprise ever!

Are We There Yet?

The Jenkins family van merged onto the highway.

"Who wants to play the alphabet game?" Liz asked her friends.

Marion, Amy, and Ellie were in the way back. Liz and her big brother, Stewart, sat in the two middle row seats. And Liz's parents were up front.

They were on their way to Marigold Lake!

"It's only about an hour drive," Stewart said. "But playing car games makes it feel even shorter."

Ellie sat up straight in her seat. "I'll play!" she said.

"Me too," said Amy.

Marion nodded. "What are the rules?" she asked.

Liz explained. Starting with the letter A, each of them had to find all the letters of the alphabet on objects they passed on the highway. The letters could be on traffic signs, license plates, or billboards.

"Liz and I usually play against each other," Stewart said. "The first person to find all the letters is the winner."

"But we could play as a team!" Liz suggested. "At least for the first game. Ready, set, go!"

Everyone looked out the window. They scanned signs for letters.

"A!" Amy called out. She pointed at a sign that said REST AREA AHEAD.

Marion found the next one on another car's license plate. "B!" she cried, clapping excitedly.

"C!" said Ellie, pointing at a billboard ad for Canoe and Kayak Warehouse.

Mile by mile, they worked their way through the alphabet. The letter J was hard to find. Same with Q.

But X was surprisingly easy. It was on every exit sign.

"There!" Liz called out, pointing to the X on the exit sign for Marigold Lake. "We're almost there!"

At the end of the exit ramp, Liz's dad turned right onto a country road.

Then, just a mile down the road, Liz's dad pulled off into a gravel parking lot. A rustic wooden sign read OTIS ORCHARDS.

Liz turned around in her seat. "We're here!" she said, grinning at her friends.

Ellie looked confused. "What do you mean?" she said. "This isn't the cabin."

Liz opened the van door and unbuckled her seat belt. "You're right," she said. "We just have to make this one stop."

They all got out of the van. Liz led the way over to a farm stand. Beyond it were rows and rows of fruit trees.

"We're going to pick fruit," Liz announced. "For pies!" Liz explained that she needed to practice baking her Thanksgiving pie. "I thought we could each bake one."

Ellie, Marion, and Amy looked at one another. Huge smiles lit up their faces.

Liz's dad came up next to them. "I made pie crusts ahead of time," he told the girls.

"So what kind are we going to make?" Amy asked.

"You each get to choose," Liz replied.

Ellie did a little happy dance. "This is going to be so much fun!"

Marion looked deep in thought already. "There are so many good pie flavors," she said. "What will I pick?"

Liz pointed at a chalkboard sign. It had a list of pick-your-own fruits that were ripe that day. "Well, you could start by *picking* some of those!" Liz said.

chapter 3

On the Farm

Liz told her friends about her Thanksgiving pie recipe.

"It's a cranberry-blueberry pie," she said. "But it's a little late in the season to pick blueberries. And cranberries don't grow around here. So I brought ingredients from home. I hope you don't think it's unfair that I had a bit of a head start."

Ellie laughed. "Unfair? I'm just so excited to be at an orchard!"

"I can't wait to bake," Marion added. Amy smiled in agreement.

Ellie studied the pick-your-own list. "Hmm. I'm going to choose apple," she said. "I just looooove apple pie."

Amy pointed to the last item on the sign. "It might sound weird. But my mom makes this great sweet potato pie," she said. "I'm going to call her and get the recipe."

Marion was the last to decide. "Okay," she said finally. "I've made a pumpkin pie before. I think I can remember how to do it."

The girls got directions from the orchard staff about where to pick. Ellie and Amy grabbed baskets to put their apples and sweet potatoes in. Marion grabbed a wagon for her pumpkins.

Then they split up. Liz took Ellie toward the apple trees. Amy and Marion went together in the direction of the pumpkins and sweet potatoes.

In the middle of the apple grove, Ellie stopped at a signpost. "Wow," said Ellie. "There are so many different kinds of apples! How do I choose?"

Liz stepped closer to the sign-post. "Look!" she said. She pointed at smaller writing under each apple type. "This one says 'good for baking.'"

"Golden Delicious!" Ellie said. "Great! I'll get some of those."

Liz and Ellie walked down the path between two rows of apple trees. They stopped near a tree that was loaded with ripe apples. Liz held the basket. Stretching, Ellie could just reach the apples on the lower branches. One by one, she plucked Golden Delicious apples and handed them down to Liz.

Soon they had about a dozen. Liz had to put the heavy basket down.

"That's probably enough," Liz said with a laugh.

Ellie grabbed one side of the handle. Liz took the other. Then they set off to find Marion and Amy.

They found them in the sweet potato section. Marion already had pumpkins in her wagon.

But Amy was looking confused.

"These are sweet potato plants," she said, pointing to the plant label at the end of the row. "But all I see are leafy vines. Where are the sweet potatoes?"

Liz giggled. She knelt down and loosened the soil around one of the plants. Then she grabbed a stem and yanked upward. Out popped a bunch of dirt-covered sweet potatoes!

"Wow!" Amy cried out in surprise. "I did *not* know they grew that way!"

Ellie put an arm around Amy's shoulder. "I didn't know how many kinds of apples there are," she said.

Marion pointed at her pumpkins. "Well, *I* do not know how many pumpkins I'll need for pumpkin pie. I sure hope this will be enough."

Marion heaved a large pumpkin
up out of the wagon. It was even
bigger than her head.

Liz, Amy, and Ellie laughed.

"That should do it," Liz said.

Chapter 4

Pie Problems

"Squee-onk! Squee-onk!"

It was bright and early Saturday morning at the cabin. The day's "alarm clock" was going off. Outside on the lake, flocks of geese honked as they took flight.

Liz rolled over in her bed. She peeked over the side at her friends in sleeping bags on the floor of her room. Ellie was rubbing her eyes.

"I forgot that sound," Ellie said sleepily.

Liz laughed. She heard giggles from inside Amy's and Marion's sleeping bags too. Everyone was awake now!

Liz looked out the window. In
the morning sunshine, the trees
around the lake were bright with
color. Lots of yellow, but also rusty
oranges and fiery reds. It was even
more colorful here than back in
Santa Vista.

"Let's go on a walk after breakfast," Liz said. "The fall colors are amazing here!"

Her friends agreed that was a great idea.

The girls got up and got dressed.

They gathered around the table in the cabin's kitchen. Liz's dad put out oatmeal and toppings: nuts, cinnamon, granola, and frozen berries. Amy, Marion, and Ellie excitedly served themselves.

Meanwhile, Liz stared at the berries. They reminded her of her pie recipe. She was really eager to start practicing.

Oh, but . . . Liz had already suggested going for a walk. All through breakfast, she felt torn.

"You know what?" Liz said when they were done eating. "You three go on without me. I'm going to stay in and make a practice pie."

Amy, Marion, and Ellie looked disappointed. "Are you sure?" Ellie asked.

"We can wait and go later," Amy suggested.

Liz shook her head. "No, that's okay," she said. "You go. It's beautiful outside." Liz didn't want to keep her friends from enjoying the lake. "I just can't wait to see how this recipe turns out."

Marion quickly switched into planning mode. "All right, how about this?" she began. "We'll go for a walk. Then, when we get back, we'll make a picnic for lunch. All four of us."

The girls agreed that was a good plan.

So Marion, Ellie, and Amy headed out toward the path along the lake. And Liz got out her mixing bowl and ingredients.

She looked at the recipe for her cranberry-blueberry pie.

CRANBERRY-BLUEBERRY
PIE

INGREDIENTS

- Blueberries
- Cranberries
- Sugar
- Cornstarch
- Cinnamon sticks
- Orange juice

CRUST

DIRECTIONS

Combine all ingredients in a saucepan. Cook over medium heat until mixture begins to boil. Stir occasionally, 12 to 14 minutes

"Sounds easy enough," Liz said to herself.

She put frozen cranberries and frozen blueberries into a saucepan. She added sugar, cinnamon, orange juice, and a bit of cornstarch.

Liz stirred it and turned up the heat. Now it just needed to boil.

"Dad?" Liz called. "Where are the pie crusts?"

Mr. Jenkins dug into a shopping bag they'd brought from home. "They're in here somewhere," he said.

He searched one bag. Then another. Then another. But no pie crusts.

Finally, Liz's mom called out from the pantry. "Here they are! I unpacked them last night."

Liz breathed a sigh of relief. "Thanks, Mom!" she said, taking one of the crusts.

Then Liz hurried back to the stove. She had to stir the berry mixture.

But before Liz saw it, she smelled it.

The scent of burning berries!

Headed South

Liz's pie mixture was so burnt it was stuck to the bottom of the saucepan.

Liz moaned. "I left it for too long without stirring!" she said.

Luckily, they had extra berries. So Liz let the mixture cool. She cleaned out the saucepan. And she started all over.

Her second try went better. She stirred the berry mixture as it came to a low boil. Then she poured the filling into the pie crust.

That's when she spotted the measuring cup full of sugar on the table.

Wait. Had she forgotten to put the sugar in?

Liz took a taste. *Bleh!* The tartness of the cranberries was overpowering. She had definitely skipped the sugar!

Liz slumped into a chair. How had she messed up *again*?

"It's okay," her dad told her. "I made extra crusts. You can try again."

But Liz was feeling too frustrated now. She needed a break. "I'll try later," she said glumly.

Just then, her friends breezed in through the screen door.

"You three are just in time," Liz said.

"For pie?" Ellie asked hopefully.

Liz shook her head. "No," she said. "To take my mind off pie." Liz told them about her mess-ups. "Let's pack our picnic!"

Liz's mom helped them make sandwiches. Amy loaded the picnic basket. Ellie grabbed the picnic blanket.

Soon Liz was leading the way to her favorite picnic spot. It was halfway around the lake on a sandy area by the water.

From their blanket, they had a clear view of the whole lake. Sun glinted off the ripples on the water. Liz took a deep breath of the fresh pine-scented air. She was feeling better already.

Liz took a bite of her hummus and tomato sandwich.

"*Squee-onk! Squee-onk!*"

Far off down the lake, a huge flock of geese took off from the water, all at once!

"Hey!" said Ellie. "You think they're the ones who woke us up this morning?"

Liz laughed. "Probably," she said.

"There must be a hundred of them," Marion noted.

They watched as the geese flew their way. Honking loudly, they whooshed overhead and kept on going.

"I think that way is south," Amy said. "Maybe they're leaving for the winter."

Ellie waved after them. "Bye, geese! Have a nice flight!"

The girls finished eating. They lounged on their blanket. Then Liz showed them how to skip stones on the water.

Finally, they headed back to the cabin.

When they got to the Jenkins' dock, Amy stopped in her tracks. "Look!" she cried. She pointed at a lone goose in the lake.

"He must be part of that flock we saw," Ellie said.

The goose stretched out his wings as if to take flight. He flapped and honked. *"Squee-onk!"*

But he wasn't lifting off. Instead, his wings were splashing water around.

The girls watched as the goose tried again. He flapped a little longer and honked a little louder. But he didn't get any air.

Liz turned to look at her friends. "Is he okay?" she asked.

Chapter 6

Goose Food

"What if he got left behind?" Amy asked.

"That flock is far away by now," Marion pointed out. "If he doesn't catch up . . ." Her voice trailed off.

"He'll miss flying south for the winter!" Ellie cried. "Oh no!"

Liz thought the goose looked a little weak. "Maybe he just needs some food," she suggested. "Maybe we should try to feed him."

But what did geese eat, anyway?

Liz and the girls hurried inside the cabin. Liz explained to her mom what they'd seen.

"Here," Mrs. Jenkins said. "Use my laptop. You can do a search for geese and their favorite foods."

The girls typed in their search. They got lots of results.

"How about bread crumbs?" Ellie asked. "Isn't that what people feed to ducks?"

Amy pointed to some text on the screen. "Actually this says that bread isn't good for ducks or geese," she replied. "It's too high in sugar. But here's a list of good choices."

- Stems
- Roots
- Seeds
- Grains
- Berries
- Insects
- Aquatic Plants

GEESE

While Amy, Marion, and Ellie read, Liz's nose picked up the scent of her failed pies. There was still a slightly burnt smell in the cabin. And nearby on the table was Liz's second failure, the sugarless pie.

The sight of it made Liz frustrated again.

She picked up the pie. She carried it out onto the porch of the cabin where she set it down on a chair.

"There," Liz said. "Out of sight, out of mind."

Back inside, Marion had an idea about goose food. "The oatmeal from breakfast!" Marion said. "That's a grain. Let's see if he likes that."

Liz hurried to the pantry. She grabbed the box of rolled oats and then ran back out into the kitchen.

Ellie, Marion, and Amy were all
huddled at the window, peering out.

"He's gone!" Ellie was saying.
"The goose is gone."

Liz ran over to see. Ellie was
right. Out on the water, there was
no sign of the goose.

"Did he fly away?" Liz asked. "Maybe he's fine after all."

Marion stepped out onto the porch to get a better view.

"Wait!" Marion called. "There he is! Liz! He's in your yard. And he's coming this way!"

Chapter 7

The Uninvited Guest

Liz opened the box of oats.

"Here!" she said to her friends. "Everybody take some." Liz poured some oats into their hands.

Then the four of them went out onto the porch. The goose was down on the lawn, snacking on grass.

Slowly, quietly, Liz led the way down the steps. They didn't want to scare the goose away.

The goose looked up at them.

"Squee-onk!" he honked loudly. The girls jumped and stopped in their tracks.

"Okay," said Liz. "I guess that's close enough!"

The girls tossed some oats in the goose's direction. They rained down onto the grass a few feet in front of him. The goose waddled over and poked at them with his bill. Then the goose straightened up. He waddled on, past the oats. And then past the girls.

"Where is he going?" Liz whispered out of the corner of her mouth.

The goose came to the bottom of the cabin steps. He flapped his wings as he hopped up the first, second, and third steps. He was going up onto the porch!

The girls followed at a distance. They watched as the goose got to the top of the stairs and then waddled right up to a chair.

The chair on which Liz had set her pie.

"Squee-onk! Squee-onk! Squee-onk!" the goose honked loudly.

"Liz," Marion whispered, "he wants your pie."

Ellie pulled at Liz's shirt sleeve. "Berries!" she cried. "Berries were on that list of foods that geese eat!"

"Really?" Liz replied. She had been distracted when the girls were reading the info. "He wants my yucky sugarless pie?"

Amy gasped. "That's perfect!" she said. "Remember how we read that bread is bad for geese? It said it's too high in sugar."

Liz laughed. "Yeah, well that pie is definitely *not* high in sugar."

Suddenly, the goose plunged his bill straight into the center of the pie. He took a huge bite of the pie filling. He gobbled it down, then took another. And another.

"He likes it!" Liz cried in awe. It was hard to believe. But that goose was clearly enjoying her pie.

The girls watched as the goose ate up all the pie filling. He wasn't the neatest eater. Globs of pie landed on the chair and on the porch and all around.

Soon all that remained in the tin were hunks of pie crust.

Then the goose turned and hopped back down the steps. He waddled calmly back toward the lake.

Watching him go, the girls couldn't help laughing. "What just happened?" Ellie asked.

"I don't know," Liz replied. "But I think I know what we should call him."

"What?" asked Marion.

Liz looked back at the messy tin. "Pie."

chapter 8

Pie's Second Chance

The next morning, the girls ate their bagels on the porch. From there, they could see Pie out on the lake. He was happily swimming about ten feet beyond the end of the dock.

"Is it just me, or does he look stronger today?" Amy asked.

Liz looked closer. Maybe he did. "We haven't seen him try to fly though," Liz pointed out.

Marion nudged Liz. "It's a good thing you baked that pie," she said. "We might not have tried giving him berries."

Liz nodded. It *was* lucky that her imperfect pie had turned out to be Pie's perfect meal. Suddenly Liz had an idea. Maybe she should make him another one?

Right now, Pie looked fine. But surely he'd need to eat again. And he'd need a lot of energy for his trip south.

That reminded her. "Do you think his flock will come back for him?" Liz asked.

All four girls looked up at the sky over the lake. There was no sign of the other geese.

After breakfast, the girls brought their breakfast plates inside. They decided to get started baking their pies. That way, they could serve them for dessert after Sunday dinner.

They gathered all
the pie ingredients.
Marion scooped
the seeds out of
her pumpkins.
Amy started
peeling sweet potatoes.
Ellie washed her apples.
And Liz decided
she *was* going to make
another pie for Pie. No
sugar. Only this time,
on purpose.

Liz was pulling out the pie crusts when she heard it.

Through an open pantry window came the faraway but unmistakable sound . . . of geese. Lots and lots of geese.

"Do you hear that?" Liz called to her friends.

Amy, Marion, and Ellie stood still and listened. The honking grew louder.

"They're coming back!" Ellie exclaimed.

Together, the girls ran out onto the porch and down the steps.

At the far end of the lake, over the tall trees, the lead geese came into view.

They were followed by many more. The flock swooped down low over the lake. In a flash, they were flying past the Jenkins' dock.

Out on the lake, Pie was flapping his wings!

"Pie!" Liz called out. "Now's your chance!"

"He's trying!" Marion said.

They watched him, holding their breath. Slowly, slowly, Pie lifted up off the surface of the water. At first, he seemed to struggle. But with each flap of his wings, Pie looked stronger and smoother. He was doing it!

"Go, Pie, go!" Ellie cried.

Higher and higher, Pie rose up into the sky. He flapped feverishly until, at last, he fell into formation at the back of the flock.

The girls erupted into cheers.

"It's official!" Liz announced. "Pie is in the sky!"

Chapter 9

Goose-berry Pie

That evening, Liz's mom and dad made veggie burgers and tofu dogs on the grill. They ate around the firepit. After dinner, they would all pitch in to clean and pack up. Then they would load everything into the van and head back to Santa Vista.

But first, they capped off their weekend with a very special dessert buffet.

Up on the porch, four beautiful pies were set out on the table. Each of the bakers was very proud of her creation. They had even named the flavors and made labels.

Amy's pie was labeled MOM'S SWEET POTATO PIE. It was her mom's recipe, after all!

Ellie's pie was labeled ASTONISHING APPLE.

Marion's was PERFECTLY PUMPKIN.

And Liz had decided to name hers GOOSE-BERRY PIE. Marion pointed out that a gooseberry was a real fruit that kind of looked and tasted like a grape. But Liz thought goose-berry was funny. As in, the type of berries a goose likes to eat.

Everyone took tiny slices of each flavor pie. That way, they could taste all of them.

Liz tasted her friends' pies first. She loved them all.

Ellie's apple pie was cinnamon-y, with a hint of lemon zest.

Marion's pumpkin pie was smooth and airy, with the perfect amount of pumpkin spice.

Amy's sweet potato pie was a yummy combination of brown sugar and ginger.

Liz took a bite of her own pie last.

She wasn't sure Pie would have liked *this* Goose-berry Pie. She had added the sugar this time. And the crust was baked to a golden brown. It tasted very different from Pie's pie.

But Liz liked it. The orange from the orange juice. The tartness of the cranberries. The sweetness from the blueberries. They went together well, she thought.

Liz looked around. Did anyone else like it?

"Yum!" said Stewart, taking a bite. "Liz, this is *good*!"

Liz beamed. That was a big compliment coming from her brother.

Ellie, Amy, and Marion nodded
in agreement. Everyone seemed to
like the Goose-berry Pie.

Even so, Liz thought she'd practice making it a couple more times
before Thanksgiving.

Just in case!

the CRitteR club

Join the club!